KENNY'S
WINDOW

KENNY'S WINDOW

by Maurice Sendak

HARPER COLLINS PUBLISHERS   NEW YORK

FOR MY PARENTS,

AND URSULA,

AND BERT SLAFF

KENNY'S
WINDOW

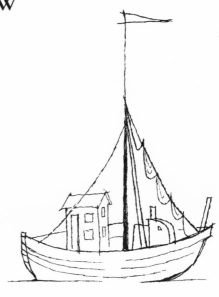

In the middle of a dream, Kenny woke up. And he remembered a garden.

"I saw a garden in my dream," thought Kenny, "and a tree."

There was a tree covered white with blossoms. And above the tree shone the sun and the moon side by side. Half the garden was filled with yellow morning and the other with dark green night.

"There was something else in my dream," thought Kenny, and he tried to remember.

"A train," he cried, "and a rooster with four feet and he gave me something."

There was a train puffing its way through the garden and in the caboose sat a rooster with four feet and he gave Kenny a piece of paper.

"Here," said the rooster, "are seven questions and you must find all the answers."

"If I do," asked Kenny, "may I come and live in the garden?"

But before the rooster could answer, the dream ended.

Kenny sat on the edge of his bed and thought about the dream.

"It would be nice to live in such a garden. In the morning I could sit in the nighttime half of the garden and count the stars and at night I could play in the morning-time half of the garden and I'd never have to go to sleep. I'll find the answers to the seven questions and—"

"The questions," he shouted, "I left them in the dream!" Kenny shut his eyes, "I'll go back," he thought, "and find them."

He turned over on his side and something crackled in his pyjama pocket. It was a piece of paper. Kenny pulled it out of his pocket.

"The seven questions," he whispered. "I had them all the time."

"I'm going to draw a picture on my blackboard," said Kenny, one morning, "and I'll call it A Dream."
He picked up a piece of yellow chalk and began to draw.
"NO!" cried an angry voice. "You cannot draw on the blackboard today."
"Why not?" asked Kenny.
"Because!" said the voice.
Kenny looked under the bed and there he found his teddy bear, sitting in the dark.
"What are you doing down there, Bucky?"
Bucky was Kenny's oldest and best friend and he slept with him every night and he had only one glass eye.

"You left me here all night," said Bucky.

"I must have forgotten," said Kenny, "I'm sorry."

"You never forgot before," grumbled Bucky.

"Don't you want to come out now?" asked Kenny. "And watch me draw a picture?"

"NO!" said Bucky. "I won't come out and you cannot draw a picture."

"I don't CARE!" shouted Kenny, and he threw the piece of chalk as hard as he could to the floor. It broke into twenty yellow pieces.

Kenny walked slowly up to the window, scraping his feet along the floor.

"What's the matter?" asked one of the lead soldiers standing on the window ledge. "Bucky up to his old tricks?"

"Last night," said Kenny, "I forgot and didn't take him to bed with me."

"Is he very angry?" asked the second lead soldier. Kenny's mouth began to tremble.

"He won't even let me draw a picture on the blackboard."

"Don't worry," said the second lead soldier, "we'll think of something."

Kenny waited hopefully.

"I have an idea!" shouted the first lead soldier. "Write him a poem about how nice he is."

"Good!" said Kenny, and he found a pencil and a piece of paper and started to think.

"How do you write a poem?" he asked.

"You think of a nice word," said the first lead soldier, "and rhyme it with a lot of other nice words until you come to the end."

"Like bear-scare?" asked Kenny.

"That's not very nice," said the first lead soldier.

So Kenny thought some more and after a lot of scratching out and erasing, he finished the poem. He said, "Thank you very much," to the soldiers and went back to Bucky.

Kenny poked his head under the bed and began to read:

FOR BUCKY

Bucky is my teddy bear.

He has short and curly hair

and on a bus he pays no fare.

He lost one eye but I don't care,

I love my Bucky teddy bear.

the end by Kenny.

Bucky didn't say a word, but Kenny felt that everything was now all right. He carefully pulled Bucky out from under the bed and laid him down on the pillow. Then he covered him with a blanket.

"Watch me, Bucky," whispered Kenny, and he walked, lifting his feet up high, to the blackboard. He picked up a piece of yellow chalk and drew a picture of Bucky sitting on the back of a rooster with four feet. Kenny turned to Bucky and said, "Do you know what you say to the rooster?"

Bucky didn't answer.

"You say," continued Kenny, " 'Can I have a ride on your back, rooster, because you have four feet and can run very fast?' And the rooster answers, 'Of course, Bucky, and when you are on my back, and I am running like the wind, you can tell me stories that only you know.' "

Bucky looked as though he was sleeping, but Kenny knew that he heard every word.

2. what is an only goat?

Kenny left a note on the kitchen table. It said: Dear mama, Am going to Switzerland. Back soon. Kenny. The valleys of Switzerland were deep in wild flowers, and the mountains peeked out through the mist. Kenny bought a ticket and took a seat in a little train that climbed straight up the side of a mountain. "Look," said a fat man, pointing out of the train window, "a waterfall!"

Everybody looked and said surprised things and took snapshots, click-click. But Kenny didn't look. He waited.

"Look, mama," said a little girl with yellow hair, "snow!"

"Ah!" said everybody. Click-click.

"Snow is very pretty," thought Kenny, "but it is not what I came to see."

And he didn't look.

When the little train came to the top of the mountain, Kenny bought a chocolate bar and went out to look for a goat. He stood in a little patch of snow and looked down into the misty valley. He listened to the faraway bells that echoed softly against the grassy-thick mountain walls.

"How beautiful," thought Kenny, "but," and he sighed, "they are only cowbells and I am looking for a goat."

Kenny stepped carefully down the mountain picking, along the way, a bouquet of wild flowers: yellow trolls, blue gentians and pink mountain roses. The path became less steep and the air smelled strong of animals. Kenny wrinkled his nose. He soon came to a village that had only four houses and a great deal of mud. "My goat could not live here," said Kenny, burying his nose in the bouquet of wild flowers. He was about to turn back, when, from behind one of the houses, stepped a little white-bearded animal.

"A goat!" cried Kenny, and he arranged the wild flowers to look as pretty as they could. Then he patted down his hair, straightened his tie and scratched some mud off his new brown shoes. The white goat watched Kenny, her little jaw swinging sideways as she chewed some grass.

Kenny stood as straight as he could and said in a loud voice, "I have come all the way from America to make you my only goat."

The white goat stepped closer, eyeing the bouquet of flowers in Kenny's hand.

"These are for you," said Kenny and he held out the flowers for the goat to smell.

"My favorite kind," said the white goat. "Thank you." And she nibbled at the yellow trolls.

"What is an only goat?" she asked.

"An only goat," said Kenny, "is the goat I love."

"How do you love me?" asked the goat.

"I love you better than the waterfall," said Kenny, "and the snowy mountains and even the cowbells."

"Ah," sighed the white goat, and she gobbled up the blue gentians.

"When will you stop loving me?" she asked. Bits of blue gentian spotted her white beard.

"Never!" said Kenny.

"Never," said the white goat, "is a very long time." And she sniffed at the pink mountain roses.

"Will you feed me yellow trolls, blue gentians and pink mountain roses in America?"

"No," Kenny answered, "but there are buttercups and black-eyed Susans in my back yard."

"Can I stand on a mountaintop in America, and listen to the cowbells?"

"No," Kenny answered, "but you can sit on the roof of my house and listen to the beep-beep of the automobiles as they go rushing by."

"Can I lie in the mud in America?"

"No," Kenny answered, "my goat must be pretty and clean and wear a silver bell around her neck."

The white goat looked sadly up at Kenny. "An only goat is a lonely goat," she said.

"But we will play together," cried Kenny, "and tell each other funny stories."

"I don't know any funny stories," said the white goat.

"Not even one?"

"No," said the goat.

"Then perhaps—," began Kenny.

"Perhaps what?" asked the white goat.

"—you are not my only goat," he finished sadly.

"That's true," said she, chewing up the last rose, "you have made a mistake."

Kenny took the chocolate bar from his pocket.

"This is for you," he said.

"My favorite candy," said the goat, gobbling it up in one bite. "And I hope you find your only goat."

"Thank you," said Kenny, and he went back up the mountain. He bought a ticket and took a seat on the little train that went straight down the side of the mountain.

From the window he saw the lovely white snow and his heart beat fast. He saw the great tumbling waterfall and he was filled with a happy longing to be home. When the train came to the station, Kenny sent a telegram. It said:

Dear mama—coming home—your only boy—Kenny.

"There is a horse on the roof," said Kenny, waking up in the middle of the night, "and I won't tell mama or papa. They would say it was a dream or what nonsense or some such thing and of course they wouldn't go up and see for themselves.

"The horse on the roof is a hungry horse because there is no more grass in the meadow. He won't eat the shingles on the roof because horses do not like eating shingles. He won't eat me because I am his friend. Maybe he'd like my fire engine or my book of big and little Indians, but I don't think so. I think he'd like to eat my cousin Harry, but he's at grandma's house and his sister Barbara cries too much.

"The horse on the roof is a lonely horse because it is nighttime, so he came to our house to sit on the roof. He makes a lot of noise but nobody can hear him.

"And he is looking at the stars. The stars make a light that you can see by and he is stamping on the roof and steam is coming from his nose. He is dancing on the roof and the stars make a light all over him. He is stamping and snorting on the roof and he is whinnying. The stars make him shiny and like velvet.

"The horse on the roof is laughing because he knows a funny story. He makes me laugh. He tells me a funny story and I tell him one. The horse on the roof makes a silly face and I make one back.

"He says, 'I must go home now. It is very late.'

" 'When will you come back?' I ask.

"He answers, 'Whenever you want me to.'

"The horse on the roof has gone back to the meadow where there is no more grass. I won't tell mama or papa. They'd say it was a dream. They don't know how to listen in the night."

4. Can you fix a
broken promise?

On Kenny's window sill stood two lead soldiers. It was night and snow was falling.

"Is Kenny asleep?" asked the first lead soldier.

"Yes," said the second, and together they began to whisper. But Kenny was not asleep and this is what he overheard.

"Let's run away," said the first.

"Where?" asked the second.

"There," said the first, looking out the window.

"That's the world," said the second, "and it's miles long. We'll get lost."

"Soldiers can't get lost," replied the first.

"Are you mad at Kenny?" asked the second.

"Didn't he promise to take care of us always?" asked the first.

"Yes," answered the second.

"Look at me," said the first, "I'm chipped in four different places. He broke his promise."

"But remember the cold night he wrapped us warm in his blanket?" asked the second.

"I remember the cold night he pushed us out of bed and left us lying on the floor," answered the first.

"And the games," said the second, "when he hides us under the pillow and pretends he doesn't know where we are. He looks in the bureau drawer and we shout, 'You're cold, Kenny.' He looks under the blanket and we shout, 'You're hot, Kenny.' He picks up the pillow and, 'There you are!' he screams and he hugs us."

"But how about the games," said the first, "when he holds us in his hands and crashes us together, chipping our uniforms and—"

"Be quiet!" shouted Kenny angrily and he jumped from his bed and grabbed the complaining soldier. He pulled open the window and laid him down hard on the outside window ledge. It was dark and snowflakes danced into the room.

"Bad soldier!" shouted Kenny, and he slammed down the window. "I never broke my promise." He began to cry. "You lied!"

The snow whirled round the soldier.

"He will catch cold," said the second lead soldier.

"Why doesn't he tap on the glass to be let in?" asked Kenny.

"He is proud," said the soldier. "And the snow has almost covered him."

"Then he's warm."

"Maybe."

"Shall we ask him?" asked Kenny.

"Yes," the soldier answered.

Kenny opened the window a tiny bit and whispered, "Are you very cold?"

The soldier's voice seemed to come from far away and it was sad. "I'm freezing under my blanket of snow."

"Say you're sorry," whispered Kenny, "and I'll take you in."

There was no answer. One snowflake landed gently on the soldier's face and covered him entirely.

"Perhaps," whispered the soldier in Kenny's hand, "he is dead."

Kenny thrust his fingers into the snow and pulled out the soldier. He was stiff. Kenny climbed back into bed and laid the two soldiers next to his face on the pillow, the frozen one in the middle. He warmed him with his breath and soon he came alive.

"I love you," said Kenny. "I promise."

"Once," said the first lead soldier, "you promised to take care of us always."

"I kept my promise," Kenny answered.

"Even when you picked us up and smashed us both together?" asked the soldier.

"Yes," said Kenny, and he sadly rubbed his finger over the four chipped places.

"Always?" asked the soldier.

"Always," whispered Kenny, "I promised for always."
The room was quiet. A clock tick-tocked.

"Look," said the first soldier, "the snow has stopped falling."

"Listen," said the second soldier, "the wind has stopped blowing."

"See," said Kenny, "the moon has come out from behind the clouds."

And as the stars appeared, they counted them one by one until they fell asleep.

One morning, Kenny almost fell off the side of the bed.

"What are you trying to do?" asked Baby, his dog.

"Almost fall off the side of the bed," said Kenny. "But not let myself just in time."

"THAT was a narrow escape!" said Baby.

"What's a narrow escape?" asked Kenny.

"Almost falling off the side of the bed," answered Baby.

"Sometimes," said Kenny, "I hold my breath for as long as I can to see what it's like. Is that a narrow escape too?"

"Be careful," said Baby, "or you'll have a VERY narrow escape."

"Have you ever had one?" asked Kenny.

"Yes," said Baby, and she shivered in memory of it.

"What happened?" asked Kenny eagerly.

Baby curled up in Kenny's lap. "For a whole afternoon," she whispered, "I pretended I was an elephant. But I couldn't sleep because I was too big to fit under your bed. I couldn't eat because elephants don't like hamburger. And I couldn't chew my favorite bone because my long nose kept getting in the way. And most of all, I was afraid you'd stop loving me. I thought, 'Kenny has lots of love for a little dog, but does he have enough for an elephant?' "

"Poor Baby," said Kenny softly, and he rubbed her back.

"And just before suppertime," continued Baby, "I stopped pretending and it was just in time. I was so hungry. And do you know what I said to myself?"

"Yes!" shouted Kenny. "You said, 'THAT was a VERY narrow escape!' "

"Right," answered Baby, and with all the talking and back rubbing, she fell asleep in Kenny's lap.

6. what looks inside and what looks outside?

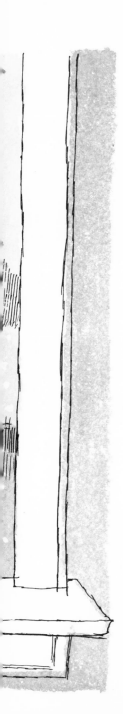

It was snowing and Kenny watched the large flakes melt against his window. They ran down the glass in long sad drips.

"My window is crying," thought Kenny. He turned his head sideways and looked up at the sky. "I wonder why snow looks dirty up there and clean down here."

"Why does it?" he asked aloud, but no one answered.

Baby lay curled up at the foot of Kenny's bed. Bucky huddled under the blankets and the two lead soldiers stared solemnly out the window at the falling snow.

"Let's do something," said Kenny. Again no answer. "LET'S DO SOMETHING!" he shouted.

Bucky's voice came sleepily from under the blanket. "Like what," he said.

"Like a party," said Kenny.

"A snowy day is a drowsy day," said Baby, and she gave a great big yawn.

"We'll make it a party day," said Kenny and he ran to his closet and pulled out his checkerboard. He laid it flat on top of the blanket. "That's the table," he said.

"Where are the guests," mumbled Bucky.

"Here are the guests," shouted Kenny, and he picked up the two lead soldiers and put them on one side of the checkerboard.

"No lady guests?" asked Bucky.

"Here's one," said Kenny and he pulled Baby out from under the bed and sat her down at the other end of the board. She promptly curled up and went back to sleep.

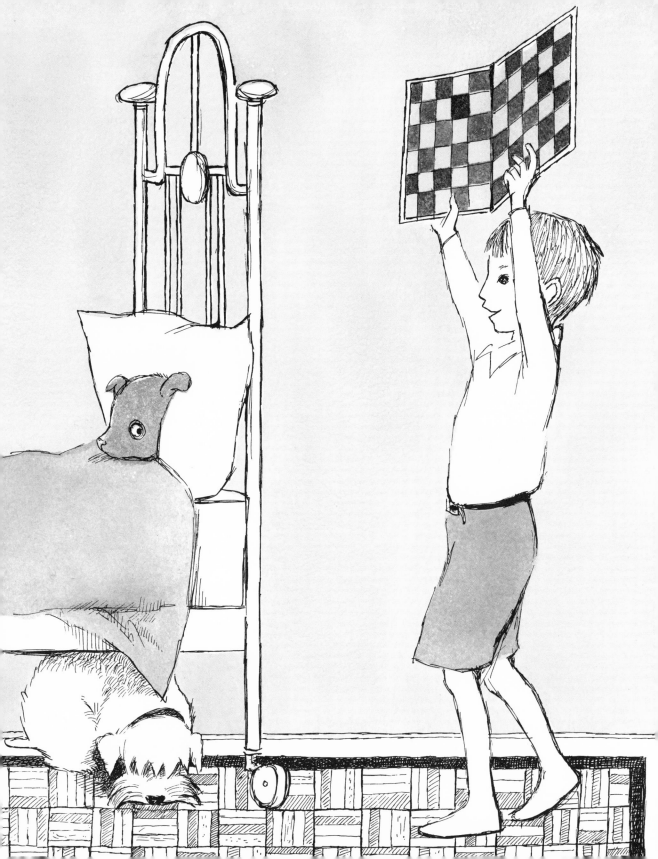

"What will we eat?" asked the first lead soldier.

"Bucky!" laughed Kenny and he laid the teddy bear in the middle of the board.

"Don't like bear meat," said the second soldier.

"O. K.," said Kenny and he sat Bucky down next to Baby. "Be a guest instead," he said.

"Thank you," said Bucky. "What will you be?"

"I'm the boss of the party," said Kenny, "AND I WANT ORDER!" He banged his fist on the checker-board and the whole bed jumped. All the guests fell down.

At that moment, the sun broke through the clouds. "Look!" shouted Kenny. "The sun is out and it's still snowing."

Kenny picked up Bucky and the two lead soldiers and ran to the window. He opened it wide and took a deep breath.

"It smells like winter," said the first soldier, "only different."

"It smells like winter is melting," said the second.

"It smells soft," murmured Kenny.

"Like spring," said Bucky.

Kenny leaned out the window and watched the children chase after the dancing snowflakes.

"You can't catch a snowflake," shouted Kenny. "They are only bits of water."

In a house across the street, a window opened and a man holding a baby leaned out. "Look," said the man, pointing with his finger, "look at the pretty snowflakes."

But the baby only laughed and pressed her finger against the man's mouth. And the man kissed the little finger. Kenny wanted the baby to see the snow too. "Look outside the window," he shouted, "outside!" But the baby saw only the man's face.

A little boy stood under Kenny's window and called, "Kenny. KEN-NY."

"That's my new friend David," said Kenny, "and I have to go now."

He picked up his jacket and started for the door. "Wait," he said, "I forgot."

He ran back to the window, picked up Bucky and the two lead soldiers and put them around the checkerboard. Baby opened one eye and thumped her tail against the pillow.

"Have a good time," whispered Kenny to his guests.

"Kenny!" called David.

"I'm coming," shouted Kenny, and he ran down the steps two at a time.

In the room, the guests were quiet. They looked at each other from across the checkerboard and couldn't think of anything to say.

7. do you always want
what you think you
want?

This was the night, the moon bright night Kenny had waited for. He was alone but not lonely. And the full yellow moon filled his room with a light that was morning bright.

This was the night that felt like the night before a big trip, scary and exciting and different.

"Tonight," thought Kenny, "I'll answer the questions in the dream." He remembered the dream.

"There was a garden with the moon on one side and the sun on the other and a tree. It was all white. And a rooster with four feet gave me seven questions to answer."

Kenny had the answers to six questions but he didn't know the answer to the seventh.

"Do you always want what you think you want?"

Kenny thought about the things he wanted. "I'd like a horse that I could ride on all around the block and even down to the ocean. Or a ship with an extra room so I can bring a friend. Or a—"

Then Kenny heard a sound. It was soft, like snow suddenly falling. Faraway, like a voice in a dream. He looked out of the window and saw, sitting on his outside window ledge, the rooster with four feet. He was smiling and beckoning to Kenny. He was saying things to Kenny. Kenny jumped out of bed and ran to the window. He pulled with all his might and the window came open.

"Can you draw a picture on the blackboard when somebody doesn't want you to?" asked the rooster promptly.

"Yes," answered Kenny, "if you write them a very nice poem."

"What is an only goat?"

"A lonely goat," answered Kenny.

The rooster shut one eye and looked at Kenny.

"Can you hear a horse on the roof?" he asked.

"If you know how to listen in the night," said Kenny.

"Can you fix a broken promise?"

"Yes," said Kenny, "if it only looks broken, but really isn't."

The rooster drew his head back into his feathers and whispered, "What is a very narrow escape?"

"When somebody almost stops loving you," Kenny whispered back.

The rooster hopped along the window ledge on three legs.

"What looks inside and what looks outside?"

"My window," said Kenny.

"And now the last question," said the rooster, "Do you always want what you think you want?"

Kenny thought for as long as he could. "I think I don't know," he said sadly.

"Think hard," said the rooster.

Kenny thought hard and then he smiled.

"I know," he said.

"What?" asked the rooster eagerly.

"I thought I wanted to live in the garden with the moon on one side and the sun on the other, but I really don't."

"You've answered all the questions," the rooster shouted, "and you can have whatever you want."

"I wish," Kenny said slowly, "—I wish I had a horse, and a ship with an extra room for a friend."

"You can have them," said the rooster.

"When?" cried Kenny. "Where are they?"

"There," said the rooster, pointing out the window.

Kenny pressed his nose against the glass.

"Across the street?" he asked.

"Further than that," said the rooster.

Kenny stood on tip-toe.

"I can't see any further than that," he shouted.

The rooster hopped on Kenny's shoulder.

"I see them," he whispered, "past the houses, over the bridge, near a mountain on the edge of the ocean."

"That's too far," said Kenny and he looked away.

"But you're halfway there," the rooster said.

In the dark, Kenny's eyes grew big. "How did I get so far?" he asked.

"You made a wish," said the rooster, "and a wish is halfway to wherever you want to go."

Kenny leaned his head against the window frame and

thought about a horse, black and shiny, and a ship
painted white.

"It's almost morning," said the rooster, "and I have
to go."

He spread his wings and flew up into the sky.

"Goodby, Kenny."

Kenny watched the rooster fade slowly into the sing-
ing lights of the city.

"Goodby," he whispered.

Kenny listened to the sounds from the city coming in through his window. They were like the songs he made up when he was happy. He closed his eyes and the sounds became a song about a horse with steam coming from his nose and silver sparks shooting from his hoofs.

Kenny fell asleep with his head against the window ledge. And the song became a dream about a horse. Kenny was riding on a shiny black horse. They galloped past houses, and people watched from their windows and clapped their hands. They galloped all over the world and even right up to the ocean. And on the edge of the ocean was a ship, painted white, and it had an extra room for a friend.

DATE DUE

MAR 3 0 2011